I0688536

Beauty Queen

Copyright © 2020 Erick Livumbazi Ngoda.

All rights reserved. Published by Worlds Unknown Publishers.

No part of this publication may be reproduced, stored in retrieval system, distributed, or transmitted in any form or by any means, including photocopying, recording, or other electronic or mechanical methods, without the prior written permission of the publisher, except in the case of brief quotations embodied in critical reviews and certain other noncommercial uses permitted by copyright law. For permission requests, write to the publisher, addressed "Attention: Director, Permissions Department," at the address below.

ISBN: 978-1-7343917-4-9) Paperback)
ISBN: 978-1-7352874-9-2 (Ebook)

This book is a work of fiction. Names, characters, places, and incidents are either the product of the author's imagination or are used fictitiously, and any resemblance to actual persons, living or dead, business establishment, event or locales is entirely coincidental.

Printed in the United States of America.
First printed edition 2020.

Worlds Unknown Publishers
2515 E Thomas Rd,
Ste 16 -1061
Phoenix, AZ 85016-7946

www.wupubs.com

Beauty Queen

ERICK LIVUMBAZI NGODA

Worlds Unknown Publishers

A Word In Advance

In January 2016, the world's biggest toy company, Mattel, the makers of the famous Barbie doll announced that they would henceforth be making dolls of different body and hair types and skin tones. These included the curvy, petite, and tall Barbie. Previously, the Barbie doll had always had the perfect body type, long blonde hair, and blue eyes. Mattel had, at last, acknowledged that beauty comes in different shapes, sizes, and colors.

Whatever you look like, you too are beautiful in your own, unique way. There is only one of you in the entire universe, which makes you so special. Always keep that in mind, no matter what anyone else says. You are perfect just the way you are!

1

The Contest

Cheryl Tate and Latoya Lami had just one other thing in common, apart from the fact that they were both thirteen years old and in the same class at Grange Academy. Their fathers were naturalized citizens, originally from Africa, which made Cheryl and Latoya second-generation U.S. citizens by birth. As for everything else, Cheryl and Latoya were at opposite ends of the spectrum. If you decided to count all the ways in which they were different on your hands and feet, you would quickly run out of fingers and toes.

Cheryl was hot—like, drop-dead gorgeous. You had to agree to that, even if you didn't like her, and most people who knew her didn't like her one bit. She was tall and long legged with gorgeous grey eyes and long eyelashes. Her creamy complexion made her look like she had an even, awesome suntan. She had been winning pageants ever since she was born. She had been a flower girl in countless weddings and even appeared in several ads for breakfast cereal, diapers, and baby formula when she was just a few months old.

Your heart would melt as soon as you set your eyes on her . . . but it would probably freeze solid as soon as she opened her mouth. She was spoiled to the core. That was probably because she was a princess—a true African princess. Her father was a king who was living in exile. Cheryl even had a title: *Batebe.* She made people aware of this at every opportunity, ridiculing them when they couldn't pronounce it correctly.

Latoya Lami's father was a software engineer and something else that was hard to pronounce. He had come to the U.S. to study on a government scholarship and had stayed after completing his studies. Latoya was short in stature and didn't not have a gorgeous figure. Most people would never call her beautiful.

Latoya was a ball of energy though. She had only been at Grange Academy for a few months, but she was already in several clubs and student societies. Then, to everyone's surprise and the annoyance of a number of students, she became the head of the student panel, in charge of organizing the annual Miss Grange Academy Beauty Contest.

Cheryl had been Miss Grange Academy for two years in a row. According to the rules, she was not eligible to be a contestant for another year. Regardless of the rules, Cheryl would hear none of it. She wanted—actually was demanding—an exception be made for her to enter the contest because she was convinced that she deserved it. Latoya was adamant that the rules had to be followed, and she was going to make sure that they were.

Both Latoya and Cheryl always had hangers-on around them—those that basked in their shadows and cheered them on. Cheryl much more on her side than Latoya had on hers. The 'groupies' happened to be around whenever any of the many run-ins between the two occurred. Like that morning in the cafeteria. Latoya had piled her tray and was heading to her corner table, flanked by Nimo Kajubo and Sarah Grey. Nimo liked both Latoya and Cheryl in different ways, but secretly felt it was cooler to be around Cheryl.

"This is neither the place nor am I the person to present your grievances to," Latoya had said dismissively as soon as Cheryl mentioned the contest rules. "My responsibility is simply to ensure that the rules are followed to the letter." She always sounded weirdly grown-up, especially when she was being assertive.

"I don't know who you are really. You haven't been here for more than a couple of minutes. We are the—" Cheryl began heatedly.

"And *who*, exactly, do you think you are, pushing everyone around?" answered Latoya, looking Cheryl straight in the face.

"If you had been around long enough to be relevant, you would know *who* I am." Cheryl crossed her arms assertively.

"Oh, I don't *care*," Latoya hissed as she strolled off towards her table, followed by Nimo and Sarah. They knew her well enough to allow her to relax and take some deep breaths before they could talk to her.

"What is this princess thing she is always yammering about?" Latoya asked Nimo as soon as Cheryl and her hangers-on moved out of earshot.

"She is a *Batebe*," Nimo answered, surprised Latoya didn't already know.

"She is a batty-who?" Latoya asked in her husky voice.

"*Batebe* . . . a kind of traditional princess back in our home country," Nimo explained.

"Oh . . . okay. I don't really care if she's Winnie the Pooh or whatever else she wants to be. The rules apply to her the same as everyone else, and we can't make exceptions." Whenever

Latoya got worked up, her lilt got thicker.– Exceptions came out like two separate words: "eyks sipshiaans."

Latoya had spent most of her life in the United States where her Kenyan father had studied and met her mother. She had enrolled in Grange Academy when her parents moved to Colorado from Tulsa. Soon after coming to Grange Academy, she had gained the reputation of being aggressive, a go getter, and a natural leader or dictator—as Cheryl and her group of friends insisted. It was sometimes quite difficult to imagine she was just a kid because she always acted so grown-up!

"She can't just drop down from the skies and start pushing everyone around!" Cheryl complained.

Cheryl descended from one of the Ugandan royal families. Her grandfather was a traditional king, and her younger brother, Roy, who also attended Grange Academy would be king one day. Her father's health was not very good, and Roy had made it clear that he wasn't interested in inheriting the title. There was little chance of them relocating to their father's home country any time soon, so perhaps Roy was never going to inherit the title. As a matter of fact, both he and Cheryl were U.S. citizens.

Cheryl had really hoped that one of her cronies, Lily Haigh or Marilyn Lipmann, would be chosen to lead the student panel. But somehow, Latoya had been selected. Cheryl had assumed that she would have no problem in twisting the arms of the student panel and the organizing committee into letting her compete and win for the third time. She hadn't planned on Latoya being chair of the student panel.

"I am a *veteran*" she'd insisted, with her habit of stressing the last word of practically every sentence, "and I have been on the student panel *twice*. I know more about the rules than *her*" She may not even know the real meaning of veteran.

Whenever she was worked up, she just said the first thing that popped into her head.

"What does she mean by veteran . . . *really?*" Latoya had harrumphed when she heard that. "You would think she was sixty-five or something. We are going to follow the rules written right here" she said, thumping the little hardcover notebook that seemed to be an extension of her very body. The rules . . . Everyone knew that in the few months she had been at Grange, Latoya had already become one of Principal Fischer's favorites for always sticking to the rules.

"Rules are what make the earth orderly," Principal Fischer always said. "They are the foundation of all order." Frankly speaking, most of the students at his school never really understood what he meant by that, but it helped drive the point home that rules were very important.

"Speaking of rules, are you going to rule out poor Libby?" Nimo asked. "She just doesn't seem . . . err . . . up to it."

"Oh . . . her." Latoya seemed to think for a minute, "What exactly did you say her problem was?"

Latoya hadn't had the chance to see Libby Knight as she had been just the previous year. As soon as she'd joined GA, her attention had been drawn to the always tired-looking girl, and at one point, she had asked Nimo if Libby was ill or something. From what Latoya had heard so far, Libby had been the only real competition for Cheryl in the past Miss. G.A contests. Everyone liked her more than Cheryl. She had the same supermodel looks. It looked like she had stepped straight out of a fairy tale. Libby had the golden ringlets and wide blue eyes that all fairy tale princesses had. For for the last few months though, she hadn't been herself. She had withdrawn into a shell and seemed to be avoiding everyone. It was unbelievable to see how much she had changed in such a short time! Having lost a great deal of weight, she was a shadow of her former self.

"Her parents have issues and it got to her somehow, I guess." Nimo shrugged her shoulders like it was really none of her business.

"Oh no," Latoya clucked, "I've heard she is quite different from the way she was."

"You can *never* imagine. You know, I'm not quite sure she isn't like, ill or something. I mean . . ." Nimo shrugged again.

The rumor going around was that Libby's parents were separating. They had been having problems for some time. Libby had overheard them arguing, although they never knew she was listening. She never imagined they would separate—until the day her dad suddenly left. The separation had affected Libby, who had always been sensitive. She had withdrawn into herself and no longer talked much, even to her closest friends at school.

"Maybe she should see a counselor or someone like that," Latoya suggested to Nimo.

"I think so too, but unless a teacher notices . . . well . . ." she shrugged her shoulders yet again.

"She is your friend. I mean, I have talked to her like once or twice, but you two seemed quite close. Why don't you suggest she talk to the students' counselor?" Latoya wondered out loud.

"Yeah, you're right actually. You don't know her well. If you did, you would know she doesn't like anyone getting into her personal stuff." Nimo lowered her tone and kind of talked through the side of her mouth in a conspiring manner, "She doesn't like anyone suggesting that something is wrong with her."

Nimo dipped her head a little, in a funny way. It really amused Latoya, but she fully understood what Nimo said about Libby not wanting anyone to treat her as if something was wrong with her. Latoya knew that feeling all too well. She had often been subjected to unkind remarks by people outside her family and when she entered school, she had been bullied. This was mostly because she was a different race from most of her schoolmates in the schools she had attended.

She had never been pretty in the classical sense, and she had been very aware of that for about as long as she had been aware of herself. She had also been painfully aware that people seemed to think that if you weren't what they thought beautiful was, then you didn't have feelings and deserved to have unpleasant stuff said to you and about you. A part of her actually kind of believed some of what the bullies said— that she wasn't as good as she should be. Then there was the part of her that strongly and angrily rejected the feeling that something was wrong with her. A part that strongly fought and resisted what everyone said about her looks.

Sometimes, she hated herself for being what she was, and other times she hated anyone that she thought was responsible for her being born looking the way she did.

The thing was, it was a personal battle that she preferred fighting all on her own, without talking to anyone about it. Who would understand exactly how she felt anyway? That was what she had always thought for the larger part of her life. And now she was certain that she had found someone else who felt exactly as she did, although she was puzzled that beautiful, perfect Libby would have any personal issues at all. She was so sure that if she had just half of what Libby had in terms of looks, why, she would be the happiest girl on earth!

"We should try to talk to her about it," she told Nimo thoughtfully. "I think I understand how she feels."

"Meaning?" One of Nimo's eyebrows lifted inquisitively,

"Oh, you wouldn't understand." Latoya caught herself just in time before she could try to explain herself to Nimo.

"What I *do* understand is that trying to talk to Libby about her issues will only make her hate you or start to avoid you," Nimo said. Libby had started ignoring her after she started questioning her about how much she had changed lately.

But that, too, Latoya understood—why Libby didn't want someone probing her with a lot of questions. Perhaps Libby had seen Nimo as one of her friends who had a perfect life with nothing to worry about getting into her personal stuff. It was a familiar feeling for Latoya.

There was the time she had caught Marilyn Saunders, whom she had thought was her best friend, talking about her with a group of other girls. Sometimes it was so hard to know who really was your friend. Most people just turned out to be frenemies—the best of buddies when you were with them but the worst enemies as soon as you turned your back.

Nimo was lost in her own train of thought. She was thinking about Ned Hall, who had been Libby's boyfriend before he suddenly left Grange Elementary. Okay . . . kind of boyfriend. Perhaps if he was still around, he could have helped Libby out of her depression. He and Libby had really been into each other. His family suddenly had to move to another state and they hadn't heard from him.

"It may not just be the stuff her parents are going through." Nimo sucked the last of her juice through a straw. "Her beau suddenly left last semester."

"Oh, he did?" Latoya asked. Perhaps she and Libby did not have that much in common after all, she thought for a moment. Latoya had never had a boyfriend. She had never thought she could have one.

2

A Silent Call

Ned and Libby's friendship had been as exciting as it was short-lived. Nimo recalled all the conversations she'd had with Libby, as she talked to Latoya. Ned was kind of shy, which she found cute and amusing. He sometimes blushed for no reason. He was so sensitive. The amazing thing was that he was on the football team. He was tall for his age and broad shouldered with curly black hair. She always looked for an excuse to be with him during recess and lunch time and after classes. The two of them had come to be known as the lovebirds by their classmates.

"It's a whirlwind romance!" Nimo had once said breathlessly to Libby.

"A *what?*" Libby had looked at her friend unbelievingly.

"Whirlwind romance, just like in the soaps. In such a short time, you two are so . . . *tight!*" Nimo had exclaimed, gesturing wildly the way she always did whenever she was excited.

"Jeez, you should stop watching those Mexican soaps, Nims, really." Libby had laughed with genuine amusement at her friend, "They are making you a bit crazy."

"But you love him! Deny, deny, *deny*!" Nimo was jumping up and down as she said that.

"You are so crazy. He's just a friend from school, just like you!" Libby insisted.

Even as she said that, she knew that Ned was more than a friend to her, but she didn't understand what had been happening to her. She had often read in fairy tales about people falling in love and beautiful princesses with long blond hair being swept off their feet by tall dark princes riding horses and living happily ever after. The lessons taught in school about the changes that happen when you enter your teens was just stuff you learned or read about. She had never really associated it with her own life until Ned came along.

Ned had been on some kind of scholarship. It was general knowledge. Word always got around. That made him the target of bullies, who saw him as a 'poor kid'—not that he seemed to care at all. He never showed a lot of his emotions. Libby couldn't remember seeing him upset or angry. She was sure he could have snapped that spindly Jonny Drew in two if he wanted. Jonny was always on Ned's case. He was part of Connor Haus's group. Connor was Cheryl's beau, and he was on the football team. He was the nastiest bully in the school.

"Aren't bullies supposed to be all fat and scary? He is more of a nerd," Libby had once whispered into Ned's ear about Jonny, in full view of the bully and his group. Ned chuckled glancing toward Jonny. Libby could tell Jonny was bothered by her comment. Since then, the tongue lashing and little pranks in the locker room targeting Ned had intensified. Shortly after that, Ned and his family suddenly moved out of town. He didn't even get to explain to Libby what had happened.

Around the time Ned moved away, Libby's parents had started having problems. Libby had withdrawn into herself, now that there was no one to talk to and share the little jokes with.

What had really pained her was that she had been unable to explain to him why she had been so withdrawn around the time she left. Did he imagine that she had been ignoring him? Libby always remembered those last days with quite a bit of guilt. She had been so down . . . but still, she should have explained to him why she was always moody. It was all so unreasonable for her to be thinking that way, and she sometimes understood that it was. But sometimes even the wildest and daftest thoughts made sense to her.

It was just as bad when she was away from school. She couldn't talk to her mother about how she felt., and there was no one else. She no longer enjoyed the movie series that she enjoyed so much before, and she often felt too tired to be able to go and hang out with her friends. Then she started eating—because it was somehow comforting. She had always loved food, although her mother often cautioned her about eating so much junk food—tacos, cheeseburgers, and such. Perhaps that was why she felt a little guilty about eating those so much, or perhaps she felt guilty because eating had replaced a lot of other things she used to do. She was afraid her weight was going to blow up. Then the other students would be up on her case like they did with fat kids-with everyone who was even a little different. Then she started making herself vomit by putting her finger or a rolled-up piece of paper down her throat. It brought some relief. Plus, she could stop anytime she wanted to . . . or so she thought. Well, she couldn't . . . as she soon realized.

She looked at the heap of chips on her plate. Her mouth watered. She just wanted to stuff the whole plate down her throat.

She would make it all come up afterwards. She had the power she thought . . . weakly because she didn't really believe that.

It was all kind of sick, and many times she had wanted to just quit it all. But it was like she had gone into it so deep—too deep to get out all by herself.

Her classmates had become used to her not eating with them. She would just go to the library and make herself busy. Even her former best friend Louisa Scott had given up trying to go past the shield of silent secrecy she had surrounded herself with lately—especially after Libby answered her well-meaning questions with rude, curt jibes. Now everyone just left her alone . . . just the way she wanted it, so she thought at the beginning. She used to do a lot of Instagram and Twitter, but she had even stopped that. Her phone was usually switched off.

Ned had wanted so much for her to participate in the Miss GA, but he had suddenly disappeared into thin air! Or at least, that's what it seemed like to her. Libby was not exactly sure what she had expected from Ned. Perhaps she had imagined that Ned would always be there. Perhaps she had imagined that the trouble her parents were having would suddenly disappear and life would go back to normal.

Libby knew it was all wishful thinking, but she still wanted to think that everything that was happening would just go away somehow, like a bad dream. Strangely enough, all around her, life just went on! Nobody seemed to care. Nights just kept turning into mornings. She had to drag herself out of bed, then into school for another horrible day, then back home again, where it was just as dreary.

People still laughed and talked and did what they had always done. The Miss Grange Academy Beauty Contest was still very much on. Now there was the new chubby girl, Latoya Lami, and she was so very much in charge.

Libby smiled feebly as she thought about Latoya: short and tubby with thick, muscular legs. Of course she could never be a beauty queen herself! Maybe she just took pleasure in pushing the girls who were taking part around. Well, perhaps she was just jealous of them. Maybe Latoya just wished she had looks and a shapely figure . . . like her. Libby sighed wearily. She wasn't going to be any shapelier, if she went on like this, she thought sadly. Something inside her kept telling her that this was all so wrong. She needed to change . . . but she just couldn't summon the energy. She looked wearily at the heap of fries on her plate, and her mouth watered again. As she got up to get the bottle of ketchup from the top of her dresser, a wave of dizziness suddenly overwhelmed her, and she almost sank back onto her bed. She was getting weaker every day. Deep inside, she just wanted all of it to stop.

"Help me . . . please" she groaned. Only her lips moved, but the words didn't actually come out of her.

3

A Matter of Choice

"A very important part of making choices is being informed," Principal Fischer said in his deep, commanding baritone voice. The hall was quiet, except for an occasional cough or the sound of someone shifting their weight on their seat or a pen cluttering to the floor. Principal Fischer was giving his weekly Friday pep talk. Most of the students of Grange Academy respected their principal, but many of them usually dozed off in the middle of his pep talks.

"I can tell what he's going to say. Why does he even bother?" Latoya overheard Linda, one of the girls from her class, complain. She didn't not find Principal Fischer's pep talks boring yet, she thought with a smile. She had noticed there was an element of repetition, but that was only because Principal Fischer really wanted to emphasize specific points.

Linda should appreciate that. She was a peer counselor, Latoya thought, and could use a lot of the material that Principal Fischer's pep talks provided.

"At each point in life, you will be faced with choices. You will be expected to choose one thing over another. There are bad choices and good choices . . . and the chances are equal that you could choose either. Now, how do you tell a bad choice from a good one? This is where being informed comes in," he continued. "The choices you make could affect your life for a long time after you made them. And sometimes once they have been made, there is no way they can ever be unmade, and you will have to cope with the repercussions— the negative results. That's why it is very important that your choices be made on the basis of information. You have to understand why you are choosing one thing over another and what are and could be the results of making that choice."

Latoya was scribbling in her notebook from time to time, much to the amazement of some of her schoolmates, who didn't see the need to take notes. She was weird like that, as far as most of them were concerned.

"Also, equally important, is to respect other people's choices," Principal Fischer went on. "Just the way you would want them to respect yours. It's a fact that everyone looks at things differently. What works for you may not work for someone else. That is why what could be the best choice for you may not work for someone else and vice versa. So, while you may not understand why someone makes the choices they have, it's important to respect the fact that it is their choice."

Latoya's mind drifted from what the principal was saying. What he had just said reminded her of what her cousin Maya had told her some time ago.

"You can choose to be happy, no matter what you are facing," Maya had told her. Maya was her dad's cousin. A true free spirit, with a loud and sunny explosion of laughter.– That was how Latoya saw her. Just thinking of Maya was usually enough to make her smile through the clouds of whatever she was going through. Okay, she did tend to yammer, and sometimes Latoya got lost listening to all the things that Maya said, but she was always a pleasure to listen to and be with.

Latoya was aware that her parents, especially her mum, didn't like her hanging out with and talking to Maya a lot, but she just loved the things that Maya said. Maya was one of the few people she could really talk to. One of the few people she really felt happy talking with. *Happiness.* That was the feeling that Latoya didn't get enough of. Latoya smiled and talked to a lot of people, but deep inside her, she had a dark hole. She had always believed that she was ugly, unlike a lot of the girls she knew. On the outside, she struggled to give the impression that she didn't care, but inside she was always so sad—and sometimes angry too. Was that the choice she had made? Could she make some other choice? Her mother always got irritated whenever she tried to talk to her about how she really felt about herself.

"Not everyone can be pretty. You're a lot of other things that other girls would like to be, but are not!" her mother had once told her, which, in a way, was admitting that Latoya was ugly.

A lot of other things? Well, she had always been at the top of her class ever since she had started school. Teachers had always described her as a natural leader. But under the confidence that everyone saw was the part of her that was sad and hurt.

"Life offers us several choices at any given time," Principal Fischer was saying. "Often there are other alternatives than the choice that was made. You choose to be one thing and not another. Here at Grange Academy, you get to choose the clubs you belong to and the person you want to be your class president or class counselor. You get to decide which of the people contesting is better suited for the posts they are contesting for.

"Almost every decision the school administration makes concerning your welfare is put to a vote, and you students get to have a say. Most importantly, you can either choose to put a lot of effort into your studies and reap the benefits in the future, or you can laze around and not pay attention and reap the consequences later on in life. At this stage of your life, most choices are being made for you by your parents and teachers. But as you grow up, you will find yourself having to make decisions and choices all by yourself."

What Principal Fischer could not possibly guess was the fact that his words had a powerful effect on the short, plump girl who was sitting at the front of the hall listening intently with a look of complete concentration on her face. This was Latoya's element, sitting there listening and not having to deal with the world outside the school. Principal Fischer finished his pep talk and prepared to leave the hall.

Latoya hoped that Connor and his group of bullies weren't waiting to pick on her. It was better when Cheryl picked on her. The boys were crueler, with their subtle innuendoes and insinuations. She closed her notebook and slid it into the side pocket of her school bag and stood up to leave.

"There she rolls," she heard someone say in a low voice. Others sniggered. Latoya felt the familiar painful throb inside her head. Her heart quickened, and she quickened her pace. She just wanted to be out of the hall and away from the bullies. Her legs felt so weak that she was scared they would give way under her and she would fall to the ground.

"My, doesn't she have such a nice round figure?" someone else said. Some of the sniggers broke into loud laughter.

Latoya could feel the tears sting her eyes. She wanted to turn and confront her tormentors, but she was sure she would burst into tears if she opened her mouth. She was sure Cheryl was part of the crowd that was tormenting her. She might have put the boys up to that since Connor was Cheryl's beau and part of her posse of bullies. Latoya tried hard to control her footsteps as she walked down the hall. She didn't want to rush because that was only going to spur her tormentors on.

"If I had a gun, I would just take it out and shoot the lot of them," she thought to herself but was immediately shocked at her own thoughts.

"Hippo!"

"Roller!"

"Ball of bullcrap!"

She could clearly hear the taunts and name calling. And she could feel her head throbbing. She fumbled with the side pocket of her schoolbag and took out her cellphone, as if she was going to check an incoming message or something like that. Her action seemed to arouse her tormentor's anger even more. To them, she looked like she didn't care about what they were saying or she wasn't hearing them. They therefore got louder and crueler. All she was trying to do was to shift her mind and focus on something else. The taunts continued, and she felt as if she was being hit by bullets. She expected to keel over and drop dead at any moment, but amazingly, she made it out of the hall. The pep talk had ended early, and it was going to be twenty minutes before her dad picked her up as he usually did in the afternoon, but there was no way that she was going to wait for that long in the school compound. She walked faster out of the school gate.

Latoya had read about how slaves were lynched in medieval times and how witches were run out of town in the history books she had read for a term paper. She thought grimly that now she understood exactly how those people must have felt. She wondered why even Nimo hadn't stayed with her to see if she was okay. She probably just didn't want to be associated with Latoya and perhaps be made the target of the bullies too.

"I'm never coming back here again . . . ever!" Latoya thought furiously as the tears finally spilled over her lower eyelids. She furiously dashed them away with one fist.

She was sure that her mother was home. She hailed a cab, certain that her mother would pay for it once she arrived.

"Are you alright, kiddo?" The cab driver's face showed deep concern as he peered at her from under the visor of his cap.

"Y . . . yes." She nodded. Her voice sounded strange even to herself.

"Are you with someone?" The cabbie looked around. He seemed very worried. His look brought Latoya back to her senses. She fished a handkerchief out of her pocket and dabbed her eyes.

"Yes, I'm fine, and no, I am not with anyone. My mum will pay when I get home." Her voice sounded normal again. She was as back in control as she could be. Even the cabbie seemed to note the change in her voice. He didn't try to talk to Latoya all through the ride home, but she noticed that he was casting quick, curious glances at her in the mirror. Latoya hated mirrors and usually avoided looking into one even when she was dressing for school or some other place. She didn't like the way her eyes were set so close together, and she always looked like the light was too strong and she had to squint to see.

She wished that at least her eyes were beautiful. Someone—she couldn't remember who—once said that they are the windows to one's soul. Latoya felt like a house with dirty windows and no one could see what she was really like on the inside. She sighed ruefully, loud enough for the cabbie to hear. She saw him cast another curious glance at her. She decided to smile just to surprise him. The cabbie seemed even more shocked at her smile.

Oh dear . . . now he must think I'm totally loony, Latoya thought. She took out her phone and texted her mum that she was on the way home. Her mum texted right back, "Is anything the matter, dear?" Latoya felt bad that she had texted her mother. She knew that her mother would be worried sick, wondering why she was coming home in a cab instead of waiting for her dad to pick her up as he usually did. As soon as the cab arrived, she just wanted to assure her mom that she was alright. Her mum knew her well enough to notice that her eyes were red and slightly swollen and she must have been crying. Cedelle Lami knew her daughter well enough to know how rarely she cried and that it must have been something really intense to make her cry. She also knew that if Latoya didn't want to talk about something, then no amount of prodding and coaxing could make her.

"Why didn't you wait for Daddy, sweetie?" She briefly touched Latoya's hair. Latoya didn't like being fondled and petted, as she always put it, as if she was part of a petting zoo.

"I just wanted to get home earlier. It has been a long day at school." Latoya shrugged as she headed straight for the stairs. Her mum opened her mouth but closed it again almost immediately.

"I have these nice muffins I just made them. Come and have some . . . when you want to," she said uncertainly, not sure if Latoya had heard the last part. There were times that her daughter didn't want to eat much because she thought everything made her fat. That was when Maya came in handy. Maya knew exactly what to tell Latoya when she was in one of her less sunny moods.

Maya. Sometimes Cedelle wasn't sure if she was a positive or a negative influence on her daughter. Positive mostly. She shrugged and went to check on the lentils she had boiling in the cooker. Maya was a bit . . . She hesitated for a moment. She thought about Maya's gaudy scarves, loud dresses, necklaces made from seeds, and exotic nature. Maya was an explosion of life, sunshine, strong perfume, and shocking words. Cedelle hadn't met a lot of her husband's people. She wondered whether more of them were like Maya. She had met her husband's mother when she visited the states, and his brothers George and Samuel, and she had often Skyped his sister who lived in Belgium. None of them were anything like Maya. They were more normal . . . ordinary.

Cedelle turned down the heat under her pan of lentils just as Maya came down the stairs. "I would like some," she said.

"Huh?" her mum said absently.

"I would like some of the muffins," Latoya said.

"Oh! Right!" Cedelle turned on her cheerful side. Latoya went over to the fridge to get a glass of juice.

"Isn't Dad back yet?" Latoya asked.

"No . . . not yet," Cedelle said. It occurred to her that Dwight could still be waiting at the school, thinking that Latoya could still be there somewhere. As if she had read her thoughts, Latoya asked, "Did you tell him that I already came home?"

"Okay, let me do that dear." Cedelle was sure the look her daughter gave her said that she thought her mother was a bit on the daft side. She kept it to herself, but her daughter sometimes had that effect on her.

"Okay," she mumbled. She was wondering if she should call Maya and have her talk to Latoya. She couldn't tell Latoya to call Maya. Latoya's voice startled her from her thoughts. She was calling her dad, and he had probably told her something funny because she laughed. Her short, brief laugh.

4

Rules Shmules!

"The rules are quite clear," Latoya explained firmly when Cheryl confronted her for the umpteenth time the next day, "You are not eligible to enter the contest this year. As much as I would like to help you, there is absolutely no way I can." She was calmer than she had been the previous day when she had had her small meltdown. If Cheryl had hoped to use Connor and his crew to break her down, then she was sadly mistaken!

"Rules *shmules.* Somehow, some way, I am definitely in. You can't stop that," Cheryl insisted. There was a whiny tone to her voice, as if she had not expected Latoya to react so firmly.

"Okay! We'll see about that!" Latoya's eyes had a gleam that clearly said as much.

"What nonsense! What are you doing on the panel of a beauty contest anyway! You look like a hipp—" Cheryl managed to stop herself just in time.

"Go on, get it out, your *royal highness*!" Latoya was almost yelling then, her hands firmly planted on her nonexistent waist, "I may look like the back end of a garbage truck, but I'm not competing. I'm in charge of the student's panel, and I'm going to carry out what I'm supposed to do, the way I'm supposed to."

"Ehmm, Cheryl." Nimo tugged nervously at Cheryl's arm. "Why don't you talk about it some other time?"

"No, we are talking about this now, once and for all!" Latoya fumed. "You will definitely not be competing this year, *your royal highness.* You are so out, and if you think I'm kidding, why don't you try me!" She was breathing rather heavily, and Nimo thought how much like an angry hippo Latoya really looked.

Cheryl took one more look at her and suddenly decided to let herself be led away by Nimo, who for some reason, was sticking with her instead of following Latoya wherever she went.

Cheryl had been a bit smug and relieved the previous day when it had seemed that Latoya was having some kind of meltdown. Her tough suit of armor was finally melting! Or so they had thought. Now she seemed stronger than ever, and determined to enforce her the rules-say-so nonsense.

"Why did you tell her she looks like a hippo?" Nimo was trying to hold back her laughter as she asked Cheryl, as soon as Latoya was out of sight.

"But that is the truth. The *nerve!* The rules, the rules, *the rules . . .*" Cheryl strutted around in an exaggerated imitation of Latoya, and Nimo almost collapsed with laughter. She didn't really like Latoya that much, and Cheryl had been her friend for much longer. Besides, her mother thought the world of Cheryl's family and always encouraged Nimo to be friends with Cheryl.

"I think you went a tad too far, though. She is still the chairperson of the S. P., you know. She can get you . . . umm . . . *ruled* out." Nimo dabbed her eyes with a handkerchief.

"I think Miss Hudson is just as fed up with her as we all are. Why can't she just go back to wherever she came from and leave us alone?" Cheryl's voice rose a bit. Miss Hudson was the teacher in charge of the contest.

"What do you have against her anyway? Is it just the Miss G. E. thing or something else? You just seem to have issues with her," Nimo pointed out. Cheryl remained silent for a moment. What her friend had said was kind of true.

"I just don't like her. That's all," she said lamely.

"You don't just not like people. You've got to have a reason," Nimo said. What she suspected was that Cheryl was so obsessed with being a princess that she really didn't like having to take orders from anyone else, especially someone that was a stranger. And to be honest, most of the G. A. students had somehow come to regard Cheryl as the royalty she was and place her up on some kind of pedestal, but Latoya frankly didn't see what all the fuss was about. And she openly showed it. Nimo was sure that was what really bothered Cheryl—that someone could actually not treat her like the princess she was. What had she been expecting anyway? Nimo wondered- for Latoya to change the rules to accommodate her? She didn't like the tension and confrontations, but some of the drama was quite entertaining to watch. She had felt really bad, though, at what Connor and the other boys had done to Latoya in the hall the previous afternoon.

"Why does she have to push us around? Do you remember when Louisa was head of the S. P.? I wish we could have her again this year or Melanie Haus . . . not this . . . this . . ."

"Hippo?" Nimo lifted one of her eyebrows as she fought the urge to laugh out loud once again.

"Well, whatever she is." Cheryl shrugged her shoulders. She was calming down. Probably coming up with some other crafty scheme, Nimo thought. Cheryl could be so vindictive, and she had a bag of tricks that she used to manipulate people into her corner. People that were not Latoya.

The only person that had ever stood up to Cheryl had been Libby, Nimo thought. Libby had somehow changed of late, though.

"By the way, have you noticed that Libby is practically fading away? What is the matter with her anyway?" Nimo asked. She had actually been closer to Libby than she was to Cheryl, or Latoya for that matter. Libby was more normal than the other two. She really missed the friendly chats she used to have with Libby. It seemed so long ago. But Libby hardly talked to anyone anymore. She seemed to just avoid everyone. And she was doing exactly what Nimo had said . . . literally fading away. She seemed to get thinner every day, and she had lost interest in just about everything she used to be excited about. As if life was slowly draining out of her.

In the strange way that people suddenly materialize just when you are talking about them, Libby appeared from somewhere near the classroom block.

"There she goes, the ghost of Miss G.A. past," Cheryl mumbled under her breath. Nimo saw poor Libby, hunched up like she now always seemed to be, as she kind of drifted slowly towards the library, exactly like the ghost Cheryl had called her.

"You shouldn't call her that *really*!" she was appalled at Cheryl's cruel remark.

"But that's what she *is*." Cheryl shrugged her shoulders dismissively. Nimo looked at her with disbelief. It sometimes amazed her how her friend could be so cold and uncaring sometimes, doing and saying things without caring how what she said affected other people. For Cheryl, everything seemed to be about her.

"And I am Miss G. E. present," Cheryl continued, totally unaware of her friend's irritation. Nimo noted that she left out the 'ghost' part when she was referring to herself.

"Nothing—not even your friend the hippo—can stop me from becoming the next Miss. G. A." There was a weird glimmer in Cheryl's eyes as she said that. Her mind reverted back to her fight with Latoya and her determination to be Miss. G. A. She didn't have a single grain of concern about Libby or what could be the matter with her.

"I can't believe you are actually saying that about Libby," Nimo insisted. She didn't like the constant attacks on Latoya either. Just because Cheryl was perfect and had everything, why did she have to be so hard on other people?

"Oh, *whatever*. Why are you making so much of it anyway?" Cheryl rolled her eyes with irritation at Nimo.

"I'm not staying here and listening to this." Nimo shook her head in disbelief as she casually strolled away. Cheryl watched her walk away, a feeling welling up from deep within her. How could Nimo dare to treat her with such insolence!

Being from her home country, Nimo should treat her with the respect she deserved. Her mother had always stressed to her that she came from a royal family. It was her destiny—her *right*—to be respected and held high above 'mere commoners'… and feared if it came to that. Even when she was just a toddler, she had always pushed the domestic servants about, sometimes making up stories about how they had mistreated her or not done something she wanted them to do, and her mother always took her side. It was only when her father was around that she had to be careful not to go too far with her tantrums and fussing. He could never stand this and would always find some way to punish her. Sometimes she grew so tired of it all. Sometimes she just wanted to be friends with the other kids . . . to hang out and laugh at silly things, spill stuff, giggle, and just be kids. Her mum had made her feel like she couldn't do those things. She wasn't ordinary. Every time she acted the way most of the other kids did, it always left her feeling like she had broken a rule or something.

"Sssup, Queen!" The voice startled her from her thoughts. It was Connor, Glen, Jonny, Nate, and their other buddy, whose name she never quite caught—the one that was always staring at her in an irritating way. She was now used to boys crushing on her, and they were usually the ones she didn't like very much.

It was Connor who was her beau. Okay kind of. He was cute and cool . . . and rude. He got a kick out of bullying and pushing other people around, but he clearly liked her a whole lot. She had read somewhere that you can tell how a potential boyfriend was going to treat you from the way he treated other people, but she thought that was all a lot of nonsense. Connor treated her like a true princess, and treated other people the way they should be treated; in Cheryl's opinion.

"Did you manage to get into the contest yet?" Connor asked her.

"I was always in the contest - she can't stop me!" Cheryl said as she pecked Connor on the cheek.

"She who? Oh! The hippo!" Connor said and laughed. His crew followed suit. Cheryl looked around with irritation. They were a crowd of idiots, she thought with disgust. If Connor told them to jump off a cliff, they probably would. But then so would some of her hangers on. Perhaps that was why they were content to hang around her, laughing at her every joke even if it was not funny, hating the things and people that she did and liking those that she liked. The ones that seemed to have minds of their own like Nimo and of course Latoya had the guts to tell her off or act the way she did not approve of.

She wrinkled her nose as the thought of Libby crossed her mind. She had been another one. Stubbornly haughty. Cheryl had never succeeded in rubbing Libby the wrong way. She just had that smug half smile on her face as if she was privy to something important that Cheryl wasn't. She never exchanged words nor forced people to see things the way she saw them. In a way she was even more exasperating than Latoya. Cheryl felt kind of relieved that Libby was no longer being such an irritation and an obstacle in the way of her being the queen that she was.

"A penny for your thoughts, your majesty?" Connor disturbed her train of thought. She didn't like the way he said that, it sounded a bit on the sarcastic side, but she knew that she had better not antagonize Connor, one of her strongest allies.

"Mmm…" she shrugged and gave him a little smile, "I was just thinking about the pageant."

"You will definitely be in it or else it is not going to happen." Connor said with a sudden grim faraway look in his eyes. Cheryl looked at him with curiosity.

"Meaning…" she shrugged her shoulders, urging him on.

"There are several ways to skin a raccoon," Connor seemed to be staring into some place far off, where no one else could see.

"Now you are getting a bit weird," Cheryl nudged him in the ribs. The crew members were also looking at Connor with knowing looks.

"If you are not in it, no pageant is going to take place."

"As in…you will sabotage the event?" Cheryl asked in a low voice.

"Shhh," Connor put his finger to his lips.

There were things that Connor could do that principal Fischer and the school administration had no idea of. Only Cheryl had a pretty good idea of what Connor was capable of. He had been part of an incident that had found itself on the front page of the local paper. Only she had known that Connor was behind the incident. He had not told her to keep it a secret in so many words, but she had somehow gotten the message.

Cheryl remembered the day very well. She had been so scared. Scared that someone would find out that she knew all along … that she was somehow involved. With time though, she had got used to the idea of keeping horrible secrets about Connor. That was what her attraction to Connor was all about mostly.

"You know how we do things, no one crosses us,' Connor drew her close and gently squeezed her arm.

"So…we are going to…like just put a stop to it?" He put his finger to his lips once again. She knew when not press him further. She was worried though, that someone could get hurt. She couldn't put it beyond Connor to hurt anyone that got in the way of whatever he wanted to do. She could feel her heart start to beat faster. Did she want to be Miss G. A. so badly? Did she really want to get Connor involved? Then the thought of Latoya strutting around and going on as if she owned the world wafted across her mind, and with it the anger that she always felt whenever she thought about Latoya. She suddenly wished Connor and his gang could do something horrible to Latoya. It would teach her a lesson or two.

She saw two of her friends making their way to the library and waved before going over to them. There was a group project they were supposed to be doing for her class. She sighed wearily. She couldn't wait for all this school stuff to be over so that she could become the model that she had always wanted to be. What was the use of learning all that history and algebra if all she wanted to be was a model?

"You may not realize it right now, but an education is one of the most valuable things you can have," her dad had often told her. She knew that it was no use arguing with him. He had absolute control over her until she was eighteen and finished high school.

There was some money from modeling ads that had been put into a trust that was going to fund her college education. She groaned at the very thought. She had to be through with all this boring high school stuff and then endure more years of college. Perhaps there was a way out. Maybe once she turned eighteen and could access her money, she could leave home and go away somewhere worth living. Deep inside, she was afraid. What was it going to be like when her parents weren't there to look out for her? As she entered the library, she noticed Latoya at a corner table. She was looking calm and collected, as if she had never had that meltdown the previous afternoon. As if all was warm and cozy with her and she didn't have a single care in the whole wide world.

5

In the Eyes of
the Beholder

"**I** have been on the phone with Miss Hudson, dear," Cedelle Lami said as she came out of the kitchen. "She says you might be stressed organizing the student panel," Cedelle said uncertainly. She had never learned how to approach her daughter, especially when she wanted to discuss something sensitive.

Latoya asked the question her mother had been trying to frame in her mind. "And you are wondering whether I want to continue heading the panel?"

"Well, if it is causing you unnecessary stress…" Latoya's mum shrugged.

"Actually, it's going to cause me a lot of unnecessary stress, but that's not enough reason to give it up." Latoya scooped some of her vanilla ice cream.

"Out of curiosity, what would be a reason that would stop you from heading the student panel?" Howie, Latoya's older brother, asked.

"If it was going to interfere with my grades," said Latoya, shrugging in a matter of fact manner.

Latoya's brother Howie was the cute one. There was no doubt about it. He was tall and slim with a creamy chocolate complexion, a heart-shaped face, and slightly brown curly hair. He had their mother's physical assets. Even the two shallow dimples that appeared when he smiled were identical to those of Cedelle Lami. Latoya was all too aware that girls would give anything to have Howie as their boyfriend—the typical teen eye candy heartthrob . . . the boyfriend that every girl wanted. And he was fully aware of that fact, which made him kind of full of himself in Latoya's opinion.

It always seemed so unfair to Latoya. She was the girl, the one who should have taken after their mother. Instead, she had their father's stocky, round appearance.

It usually cut deeper when Howie innocently did or said anything that made her feel bad about her looks. The day she had discovered that she had well-defined sideburns had been one of her lowest. She had been trying to squeeze a zit on her forehead when she noticed the unmistakable dark outline on her cheeks. The only person she could think of telling was Maya. She knew her mother would impatiently dismiss her fears and tell her not to spend all her time worrying about her appearance. Latoya thought it so unfair, because her mother never had to go through hell because of her looks. Her dad would only laugh about it because he would think it was hilarious and she would never hear the end of his good natured teasing. He was the one person who liked the fact that his daughter was his exact replica physically, except for the fact that she was a girl. It had been Maya who had taught her how to wax her cheeks and get rid of the hairy outline before anyone noticed.

Maya was the typical artist who saw things that other people did not. She painted and also did spoken word and poetry. Tall, dark, and incredibly slim, she kept her head clean shaven at all times and always wore huge hoop earrings, gaudily colored outfits, and bright red lipstick. Latoya knew that her mother found Maya's constant loud talk, weird mannerisms, and bray-like laughter a bit annoying, but her father didn't mind at all. Latoya just loved the warmth Maya brought into every room she entered.

Latoya knew she could ask Maya anything and get the exact answer she needed. And, in fact, it was to her friend that she went the day Cheryl had called her a hippo. Latoya had learned to conceal her true feelings from the time she was a kid. People often made cruel remarks about her appearance, about as much as they talked about how cute her brother was. What had hurt her most about Cheryl's insult was that Howie had once also compared her to Gloria the hippo, a character in the animated movie *Madagascar*. They had been watching it with their parents when he had just said it innocently. "Hey Latoya, the hippo looks just like you!" Everyone had laughed, and she had pretended to find it as amusing as they did, but as soon as she could, she had gone to her room, lain face down on her bed and cried for hours. Latoya was sure that her brother never meant to hurt her, but it still hurt horribly.

Latoya's outgoing nature made everyone think that she didn't care about her physical appearance and wasn't self-conscious at all. But inside, she was sensitive and easily hurt, especially since she didn't find it easy to confide freely in people, except for Maya.

"It's so unfair", she told Maya that evening.

"Life itself is not fair, dear, and it is not supposed to be!" Maya told her in her usual cheerful, loud voice.

"Why did God swap our looks? He gave me the wrong face. Howie is the boy. He's the one that was supposed to look like our dad." Latoya couldn't stop the words from tumbling out.

"He did not switch your looks around. He had a purpose, and He intended you to look the way you do." Latoya had always found it amusing that Maya talked about God in the most touching manner, yet she never stepped inside any church.

"Then He must be very cruel. Why did he make me look like a . . . a . . ." She just couldn't bring herself to say hippo.

"He has a reason for doing everything. God is an artist," Maya said.

"Oh, He is?!" Latoya actually started grinning through her tears. That was the effect Maya always had on her.

"Yes, really!" Maya had insisted "Have you ever noticed that not all the pieces I paint or mold are exactly beautiful in the way most people would define beautiful?" Latoya had looked around Maya's studio. Some of the sculptures and paintings were simply monstrous, to put it simply. She looked at a painting of a woman who seemed to have horns and a nose above her bulging eyes. Weren't all paintings supposed to be of beautiful things? Things that people would love to look at all the time and hang on walls or prop up on mantelpieces to show them off to others?

"You see?" Maya seemed to have read her thoughts. "Beauty is in the eye of the beholder. What you may find physically appealing could be, to someone else, very unappealing. Beauty lies deeper than what one can see just by looking on the outside. It's in the tale that something has to tell. What lies deep within it . . . and only those who have the inner eyes to see it can understand."

"Wow, that's kinda deep, isn't it?" Latoya was actually grinning openly as she said this. She had always liked the way that Maya had of stringing words together.

"This Miss G. A.," Maya started after a long pause.

"Yeah." Latoya could feel that Maya had something up her sleeve.

"I was wondering, instead of just heading the student panel, why don't you sign up and enter the contest?" She reached out and patted Latoya's head as she said that. For a moment, Latoya just looked at her friend, her mouth open with surprise, and then she broke out into loud laughter. Coming from anyone else, she would have found this deeply hurting. But from Maya, it was definitely a joke. It was only after she had stopped laughing and dabbed her cheeks with a handkerchief that she looked up and noticed that Maya could not have been joking.

"Did I say something funny?" Maya asked, putting on one of her rare serious faces. Latoya looked at her uncertainly, "I don't think you understand . . . it's a *beauty* contest."

"Of course, I know what it is. That is why I was asking why you haven't considered entering the contest," Maya said without batting an eyelid.

"Are you trying to tease me?" Latoya asked after a while, looking at Maya quizzically.

"What is your idea of being beautiful anyway?" Maya asked her in a serious tone

"Well, there are rules, and the reason why I am very unpopular is that I might have been just a little bit too vigilant in enforcing them. But the unwritten rule, of course, is that one has to be . . . well, *beautiful!*" Latoya explained. There was a category for the most well-dressed contestant, the most beautiful eyes, and the most beautiful outfit, but Latoya just grew tired of explaining it all to Maya.

"What!" Maya seemed genuinely surprised, "That is a totally outrageous concept of beauty, especially since you are all kids. Your physical beauty hasn't even formed yet!"

"Well, those are the rules, and I most certainly don't qualify." Latoya shrugged. She wanted to point out that even so, there was actually no way that she was going to be growing any more beautiful when she got older—probably even uglier than she was at that time—but she just couldn't bring herself to form the words.

"How *absolutely* ludicrous! Anyway, rules can be changed you know . . . especially if, as you said, not a lot of people seem to like them. Can't you just talk to someone about getting them changed? Maybe the teacher in charge or the principal?"

Maya could make things sound so easy when she talked about them. Latoya warmed up to the idea immediately. She could talk to Miss Hudson about it. Why not? Maybe then, Cheryl and her friends wouldn't hate her so much. Well, at least there would not be any harm in trying. And about her entering the contest . . . well, everyone would laugh, but they already did, so would there really be any loss?

There had to be other ways to run a beauty contest than what had always been done before. The rules had remained unchanged for years . . . decades. She had heard Principal Fischer say something like that when she and the rest of the student panel had been selected.

That evening, while she talked with her mum and brother, the idea suddenly grew firmer in her mind. What if there were other things that were judged in the contest, apart from physical beauty? There should be other ways in which someone can be beautiful apart from having a well-proportioned face, nicely shaped cheekbones, and spindly
gs.

"You are kind of scary when you're thinking so deeply," Howie said. Their mother smiled, without saying that she thought exactly the same thing.

"Well, I *am* thinking," Latoya said mysteriously.

"Evidently," Howie gestured with his arm impatiently, so that she could just go ahead and tell them what it was she had been thinking about.

"I shall be resigning as the chair of the student panel." Latoya got it all out at last, and actually sighed deeply as if a burden had lifted. Howie looked genuinely perplexed. Their mother didn't seem to understand what her daughter had just said. She had really been wishing that Latoya could give up on the whole idea of being the head of the panel, but she just didn't think it was possible to convince her to quit. When what Latoya had just said fully dawned on her, Cedelle dropped the dishtowel she had been holding and rushed to engulf Latoya in a tight bear hug. Her relief was so obvious. She usually didn't show her true feelings. Her relief was short-lived. It lasted only until Latoya dropped another bombshell.

"Yes. But I'm entering the contest for Miss G. A."

Her mother's mouth dropped open and she stepped back from her. Actually, the looks on her mother and her brother's faces were identical for one long minute, until Howie laughed loudly before he could stop himself.

"Howie!" their mother quickly said in a choked voice. It was hard for her to process what Latoya had just said. She wasn't sure if it was a joke they were supposed to laugh at or they had misunderstood what she said.

"What did you say, dear?" she asked again, looking intensely into Latoya's eyes. Every cell in her body strained with the effort of willing her daughter to say it was just a joke, and of course she would never do such a thing. Cedelle was horrified of the ridicule that her daughter was definitely going to face if she decided to go through with such a crazy idea.

"I said I am entering the contest for Miss G. A. this year now that I am no longer on the student panel." Latoya said this slowly and clearly so there would be no mistake about it. Cedelle took a deep breath. She drew back one of the chairs at the dining table and sat down, breathing deeply so that she could think clearly.

"Honey . . . sweetie . . ." she began carefully.

"Are you serious?" Howie finally found his voice, and realized that his sister was dead serious. He rolled his eyes and turned to their mother.

"Mum, can someone resign from being a brother?" He groaned, half serious. He just didn't want to be part of the negative attention it was all going to bring their way.

"Wha . . . you don't quit. I fire you from being my brother. Whatever." Latoya actually laughed out loud as she said that. She was so relaxed about the whole thing. They hadn't seen her so carefree and jovial in a long time. Her mother looked closer a her, her face creasing more deeply with concern.

"Honey…" she tried again, gently putting her hand on her daughter's shoulder but not getting any further.

"No, I haven't snapped or something. I've got this." Latoya gently took her mother's hand off her shoulder, having accurately read her thoughts. Mrs. Lami was wondering if all the stress had finally gone to her daughter's head. She wasn't exactly sure it hadn't. She made it a point of getting her dad to talk to her as soon as he got home. He was better at these things.

Latoya tried not to show her disappointment over the reactions. She could see from the corner of her eye the kind of glances that her brother was casting her way, like he was wondering which way to run if she suddenly lunged his way. The only person who would understand would be Maya. She was all for crazy ideas.

"All ideas seem crazy at first until they work out," she had once said.

Latoya wondered if Maya was free at the moment or engrossed in one of her projects. She took her mug and plate to the sink and made her way to her room. She noticed that her mum and Howie were still staring at her, probably afraid of saying something that was going to set her off.

"Honey, I am so thrilled for you!" Maya was genuinely pleased. It was so obvious. She had no hang-ups like everyone else Latoya knew. She was so thrilled that she actually screamed and whooped! And it wasn't just that she had been a positive influence or that Latoya had taken her advice seriously. She was simply thrilled that Latoya had the courage to venture down such a daunting path.

"We should start working up a strategy straight away! I'm coming right over!' Maya trilled. Did she mean like right over to her house? Drive the twelve miles from where she lived just to help Latoya create a strategy? Latoya was about to tell her not to go to so much trouble, but she thought better of it. She was just the person to help her convince her parents that she needed to do it. How important it was for her that it be done.

She started checking out the website links Maya had sent her immediately after they finished talking. There were amazing stories from all around the word. The stories of inspiring people who achieved great things despite the lack of support from those around them. People who went ahead and did what they did anyway—and succeeded. There were also stories of people who hadn't been thought beautiful in the way that most people perceive beauty, but they went ahead and achieved a lot in the fashion and beauty industries. Latoya especially loved the story of the African supermodel who had been described as "hideous" and "disgusting" by a lot of people just because she didn't fit what their idea of what it took to be a supermodel, but she had soared above all that and achieved success beyond everyone's imagination.

6

A Positive Influence

"I choose to be beautiful," Latoya made the startling announcement suddenly, smack in the middle of dinner. It was two days after she had made the big decision. It was so sudden. Her dad had been explaining something complicated to do with politics. He paused for a moment, with his fork, which he'd been gesturing with, poised in the air before he gently lowered it to his plate.

Cedelle slowly put her fork down, swallowed the food she had been chewing, and looked at her daughter. Sometimes her daughter said the strangest things, and she had learned from experience to think carefully before she responded in any way. She had always suspected that the child had a higher IQ and a deeper thinking process than her. She hadn't even wrapped her mind around the fact that Latoya was going to actually enter a beauty context. A science exhibition or a spelling bee she would understand perfectly and know how to be supportive about . . . but a *beauty* contest?

"What did you just say, dear?' she asked slowly.

"I said I have decided to be beautiful. I won't think of myself as ugly anymore," Latoya repeated. Howie snorted and pretended he had choked on some food. Their mother gave him a *don't you dare* look, and he immediately started staring at his food.

"But you have always been beautiful, angel!" Dwight Lami laughed uproariously. "I have told you countless times that you look just like my mother, Nyar K'Ombewa as they used to call her. And she was said to be the most beautiful girl in the village during her time."

"Oh, spare us all that." His wife flapped one of her hands. She had heard enough of the legendary Nyar K'Ombewa's praises throughout the course of the seventeen years she'd been married to her son, Dwight Eisenhower Lami—enough to last her five lifetimes.

"Latoya, to us you have always been beautiful. It doesn't matter what you choose." She patted her daughter's hand.

Howie rolled his eyes. He couldn't remember when his parents were so encouraging and sweet to him. He had never needed it, even though he was three years older than Latoya.

"I'm going to my room to watch a soccer game," he announced as he pushed his chair back. "I have chosen to be David Beckham," he added and hastily made his exit before either of his parents could say anything.

"Don't mind him, dear," Cedelle quickly told her daughter.

"Yes." Dwight looked around shiftily before leaning forward and winking at her in a conspiratorial way. "He can hardly tell a soccer ball from a bar of soap." Latoya laughed out loud at her father's clowning. She knew they were trying to make her not take Howie's teasing too badly.

Dwight wasn't lying about his late mother. Okay, he did exaggerate now and then, but his mother had been considered beautiful by the standards of her people. She had what is often described as a full figure. He had inherited her rather short stature, child bearing hips, the broad face, and almond shaped eyes from her. And most of this, he had passed on to his daughter, a fact that he was very proud of.

In their culture, that was beauty! Other people would see beauty some other way but that was the way his people chose to see beauty. That was what Latoya was trying to show. She had adopted a new attitude; it was a total paradigm shift. She was to going to show the world another angle from which beauty could be seen. The hours she had spent on the internet downloading and reading information about unconventional beauty had paid off and infused her with a confidence that she had never felt before.

Principal Fischer's pep talk about how one chooses and charts one's path through life by deciding how to look at life constantly came back to her mind. She would no longer feel bad about herself on the inside while showing the world a face of bravery. She was going to be as brave and confident on the inside as the face she showed to the world.

Cedelle, on the other hand, had always been secretly worried about her daughter's lack of physical appeal, as she saw it, and had waited with dread for the time this would start affecting her daughter's self-esteem. She had seen from the first day that her little girl took a lot after her father. When Howie had been born with most of her looks, she and her husband had both been very amused, with Dwight remarking that the angels putting him together probably made him a boy by default when they had set out to assemble an exact replica of her. But when Latoya was born three years later, Cedelle had been filled with this strong foreboding. She remembered how physically unappealing girls had been taunted and teased when she was a school girl. She just didn't want her daughter to go through such trauma.

"So!" she drove the thoughts from her mind and smiled at her daughter again. "What made you think of that?" Latoya's dad leaned forward again to listen better. He was also wondering what had made his daughter make such a choice.

"Well, something that Principal Fischer said some days ago. But it seems like I have known it all the time", Latoya explained. "He said that life is a matter of choice. A lot of the time you are faced with choices, and what you choose determines your happiness and perhaps success in life."

Latoya's mum had never been quite a fan of Principal Fischer. She could not explain why, but he reminded her of an incident she had during her own school days. Her mood altered slightly when Latoya mentioned him.

"Mom?" Latoya startled her out of her thoughts.

"Huh?" Her husband was also looking at her in a curious way.

"Did you hear what she just said, Cedie?" Dwight asked with a slight frown on his face.

"Yes, dear. Principal Fischer . . . you were saying what he told you."

"Yeah, and it got me thinking, if my self-image could shift sharply to the other side from what it has always been, then no matter what anyone else sees, says, or thinks, my image of myself would firmly remain."

Her parents turned to each other, the looks of surprise on their faces almost identical. Sometimes the things their daughter came up with just freaked them out. Dwight was the first to recover.

"Why, good for you!" he exclaimed, searching for the right words as he spoke. "But to me, you have always been the most beautiful little girl in the whole world," Latoya looked at her mother. Cedelle was quietly staring at her plate, still trying to digest what her daughter had just said.

"Mom . . ." Latoya said quietly.

"Huh?" Her mother looked startled.

"Have I also been the most beautiful girl to you too?" Latoya was watching her mother's face intently, as if she was trying to figure out if she was going to lie to her. "You always say I shouldn't worry about being beautiful, but you have never told me if you think I *am* beautiful."

Cedelle dabbed the corner of her mouth with a napkin before slowly putting it on her empty plate. She noticed that her husband was trying to hide an amused smile. Her daughter wasn't beautiful in the way that everyone else defined beauty, but then, being beautiful didn't always make one happy. She understood that all too well.

"It doesn't matter to me whether you are beautiful to other people or not dear . . . I love you just the same . . . and yes . . . to me you are the most beautiful girl *ever*." She gently patted her daughter's shoulder.

The way she said this, and the look she gave her, was all that Latoya needed at that time. Now, no matter what everybody else thought or said, just the thought that both her parents thought she was the most beautiful girl *ever* was going to be uppermost in her mind.

*****

Cedelle was quite grateful that Maya had helped to bring about such confidence in her daughter. She hadn't been a fan of Maya's. She thought that Maya was too artistic and too bold to be an influence on her daughter. And there was also something that disturbed her about Maya, but she didn't want to even discuss that. Her constant worry was whether it was going to kind of rub off onto her daughter . . . or that she was going to influence Latoya into it.

"She has all the right to be whatever she wants to be, as long as it doesn't rub off on my daughter," Latoya had overheard her mum say one day.

"Dear, I'm sure Maya knows better than to influence our daughter *negatively*," Dwight had answered carefully.

"Oh, I know you always take sides with her because she's your second cousin four times removed or something like that". Cedelle had always snorted at the family system of her husband's ethnic community. Everybody from her husband's village seemed to be his close relative.

"You don't have to be facetious, Del. Actually, Maya's father and my maternal grandmother's—"

"Oh, *please* kindly spare me the branches and twigs of your family tree. What I want you to talk to her about is the influence she could have on my daughter, and to keep her personal habits to herself." Latoya had not been very sure what her mother meant by Maya's personal habits. Perhaps it was her loud talk and her braying laughter or something like that.

"But dear, Maya has been nothing else but a *positive* influence on Toya, as far as I've seen . . . and I don't think Toya is old enough to start getting interested in . . . you know what . . ."

"She's no longer a baby; she is sixteen, Dwight. thirteen.— A *teenager* . . . an age when they get easily influenced."

"Okay, you talk to Latoya. It's mothers who are supposed to discuss such things with their daughters. I will see how I can make Maya understand your fears."

"Just *make* her understand."

Dwight knew that it was time to stop trying to reason further. The conversation had made Latoya wonder a lot. She didn't know how she could ask her parents about what they had been talking about without letting out the fact that she had overheard their conversation, kind of eavesdropping on them, which was something they really frowned on. Now that they were even closer, thanks to her intention to enter the contest, she wondered whether it was the right time to ask Maya directly what it might have been all about. But then she was going to have to let her know that her parents had been discussing her, which just wasn't cool.

She had been in her room thinking and bracing herself for the backlash she was sure to be facing the next day, when she was going to make her announcement. When she made her way downstairs into the lounge, she found Howie and their parents watching a movie. Her father always said that watching movies was something that idle people did. He would rather watch reality features; National Geographic and the like.

"Why spend so much time watching something fictitious, that never happened?" he always asked in his booming voice. But he never stopped his children from watching them, and Cedelle enjoyed good movies—especially romantic ones. Cedelle and Howie sat on poufs, watching *Jumping the Broom*. Dwight was actually pretending to be reading one of the dailies and trying to look gruff and distracted. Howie noticed to his amusement that his father would peer from around the newspaper from time to time and watch the movie for some minutes before ducking back behind the paper once more as soon as he sensed that someone was watching *him*.

Howie was coming to find that his father's antics were more interesting than the movie itself when his phone suddenly buzzed. The sudden sound startled him so much that both his parents and his sister looked at him with surprise. It was Connie. Howie had been expecting the call for a while, but as soon as it came, it threw him so much off balance that even his father noticed that something was amiss.

"Eeer . . . excuse me," he muttered half to himself as he hurried out of the room. Dwight looked up and noticed that both Latoya and her mother were staring at Howie with half open mouths. Howie had never done anything like that. He would always take calls, which were usually from his school buddies, in the presence of everyone. And none of them had ever noticed him betting all flustered about a call.

Dwight ducked behind his newspaper again so that the girls wouldn't see his smile. Latoya noticed that her mum also seemed mildly amused, and she probably wasn't saying anything about what had just happened to her dad because Latoya was present.

"What just happened?" Latoya asked with broad grin.

"Your brother finally has a girlfriend, that's what!" Her dad finally found the outlet he had silently been looking for, and burst into gales of laughter.

"Come on, Dwight, you don't know that!" Cedelle said. But Latoya noticed that her eyes were dancing and glistering with suppressed laughter.

"You know very well that's what it is!" Dwight roared with more laughter.

"Soon it will be our little girl with a beau of her own!" Dwight slapped Latoya slightly on one shoulder. Latoya could feel her cheeks burn, and she covered her mouth, smiling shyly.

The couple of minutes that it took her to look up again were enough for her mother's mood to change noticeably. The smile froze at the corners of her mouth, and the look in her eyes changed.

Latoya's laughter dried up too as soon as she noticed the look in her mother's eyes. Her dad's loud laughter and cheerful chatter also dried up.

"But I will not ditch my parents for any boy!" Latoya slapped her palms together and said in a cheerful voice. Could they just have been worried that when both their children found their true loves, they would abandon them? Her father broke into uproarious laughter again. She was so happy that she had at least diffused the awkwardness. Her mother smiled uneasily too, but Latoya noticed that hers was the kind of smile that didn't show in the eyes. She couldn't figure out what it was, but somehow, she felt hat the awkwardness her dad's words had caused was connected to the conversation she had overhead them having about Maya.

"Speaking of which, I think Howie will have to be my chaperone at the contest," she said in a kind of excited tone. She noticed her mum's face kind of fall even more.

"Are you still going on with that, dear?" Cedelle asked in the small voce that she used when she was very worried.

"She sure is going ahead with it, and she's going to win that contest. There can't be anyone more beautiful than she is!" Latoya's father flapped his newspaper towards her mum.

Latoya wished she had half as much confidence in her beauty as her dad apparently had. She didn't expect to win the beauty pageant. She just wanted to make a point. She didn't like the way the likes of Cheryl and her group of cronies were so hung up on what they thought was beauty and how they were all that beauty was. She just wanted to stir the water a bit—cause some ripples. Perhaps when all was said and done, she would have created a totally new way of looking at things . . . or she would be laughed out of town. Whichever way it was going to go; she was ready to face the music. Thinking of facing music, she thought of the superstar that

Maya had told her about. The first producer she approached had said that she sounded like a she-goat and had better find something else she could do with her life apart from music.

Latoya smiled as she remembered the way Maya had told the story. The musician's voice was a bit sultry, and she sounded a bit different from the way other musicians did, but she made it big in the music industry just the same. People get repulsed by things that are extraordinary—that shift away from what they have always known. Once they get used to a new idea or a new appearance, perhaps their minds open up and they learn to accept it more.

"New fashion trends seem hideous when they roll out, but with time and enough marketing, they became the rage all over the place!" Maya said. Latoya thought of the ragged distressed jeans that a lot of her schoolmates wore. Her dad sarcastically called them 'stress jeans', and Howie wore them a lot too. To all appearances they seemed like the wearer had gotten into some kind of catfight and someone or something had torn their clothes off, but to the fashionable, they were the in thing.

Latoya was startled from her thought by her phone ringing. Nimo? She was a bit surprised at getting a call from Nimo. They weren't exactly the "call each other and chat for hours" kind of friends. Latoya didn't have many of those.

"Err . . . Hi!" She tried to sound very cheerful as she answered the phone.

"Is it true that you have been thrown off the S. P.?" Nimo sounded a bit worried. Maya quietly groaned and rolled her eyes. The rumor mill was grinding already.

7

𝔓utting it to 𝔙ote

"Well, we could run a referendum and, you know, let the people have their say!" Principal Fischer seemed quite excited as he said that. He was speaking with Latoya and a very worried-looking Miss Hudson. Latoya would have sworn that Miss Hudson looked older than she usually did. Actually, she was younger than Latoya's mum. Latoya was sure of that. Ms. Hudson was always humorous and friendly. Her smile had not been seen for the last few weeks though. Latoya wouldn't have known it, but Miss Hudson had been trying to convince Latoya's mum to prevail on her daughter not to be in the beauty pageant. There was also something else that she couldn't confide even to Principal Fischer—something that was making her sick with worry.

"Do we have time for that really?" she asked in a very uncertain voice.

"Come to think of it, we don't really have much time, but then this is a school—a place where we should be learning and trying new things …and new ways of doing

52

old ones!" Principal Fischer tapped his fingers on the table, deeply engrossed in thought.

"Well, there is always a way around obstacles." He finally seemed to have thought of an idea. "As the president of this institution, I can issue an executive order bending the rules around the pageant to accommodate good ideas… all for a good cause." He seemed to be adding the last part for his own assurance. It wasn't a thing that was done—that had ever been done before—but as he always said, there has to be a first time for everything. This was definitely going to be a first. The students were usually given the chance to have the final say in most of the major decisions that were going to affect them in one way or another.

"Our mission is to send you out there into the world fully prepared for everything you may encounter. Including processes and procedures that may be required of you as citizens of any country," Principal Fischer always emphasized.

The school had a panel consisting of a representative from each of the four streams of each class and each class teacher. This was called the joint elections panel, which oversaw and sought to ensure that elections were done fairly, according to the rules of the school. That included any referendums that were held within the school. This time, there was no time for a referendum, and a heated push and pull was no doubt going to occur. It was a time for someone with heavy shoulders to exert some force and push things along the way.

Soon, word about Latoya's resignation from the student panel was stirring up the wheels of the gossip mill around the school. Lily Haigh was replacing her, and Cheryl Tate should have been celebrating and breaking out the champagne, figuratively, but she still had a bone to pick

"She saw the light on the way to Damascus or something?" She sneered skeptically as soon as she and the girls who always tagged after her had read the notice on the bulletin board.

"What are you complaining about? It was you who was so much anti-the-rules," Nimo asked.

"Yes, but when a lion suddenly turns vegetarian, you have to get cautious, you know." Cheryl's expressive eyes widened slightly.

"How human." Louisa Wagner tossed her long ponytail. "Always finding something to complain about." Louisa was one of the girls who held Cheryl up on a pedestal.

"But haven't you read the notice properly?" Cheryl snorted with derision, "The hippo wants to enter the pageant!" All the other girls burst into laughter. Those who had seen that part of the notice had probably thought that they'd read it wrong. It didn't make any sense. Perhaps Miss Glass, the principal's secretary, had written that by mistake. Or was it meant to be a prank?

"Perhaps someone is trying to have some fun with her, or us," someone in the small crowd said.

"No, if the rules change, then people like her would be able to enter the contest." There was a whiny note in Cheryl's voice as she said that. It was quite clear in the way she said it that she considered herself as belonging to a group of people that held the exclusive right to enter beauty pageants—a group that Latoya did not belong to.

"Oh, please. It's supposed to be a *beauty* contest. Latoya may be any number of things, but beautiful? *Naaaah!*" Celia Clarke pointed out.

"She certainly is a nice round figure," one of the other girls said, and they all burst out laughing.

"But that's just it. She's out to change the rules, and it will no longer be about beauty!" Cheryl said in a plaintive voice.

Nimo rolled her eyes. She was about to point out something that they had often heard in Principal Fischer's pep talks: that when all that you have going for you is your face, that will fade with time, but if what you have going for you is inside your head, then you have a treasure that will last you your entire life. Nimo had never considered herself much of a beauty, but then she had never thought of entering pageants either. Those were things that other people did. She thought that what she had going for her was inside her head. Her grades were above average, and she was the favorite of one or two teachers. She wanted to study law and be part of her dad's firm after college, not go strutting around on catwalks. That was what made her want to be close to Latoya sometimes, although all the negative vibes that everyone else sent towards Latoya were enough to scare her from being her friend.

"Please," she drawled. "I have known all along that whatever you have against Latoya has nothing to do with the pageant rules. You're now complaining because she has suggested that the rules should be changed. Being able to enter the contest is just what comes with the changing rules."

"Whatever," Cheryl retorted. "This is just one of her tactics. She wants to get the entire thing rigged, and she will do that over my dead body!"

"Wow, I will hate to be the grass under your feet when you two elephants fight!" Nimo held out her hands.

"She's the elephant, not me!"

"Just a figure of speech. Don't get me wrong," Nimo said as she made her escape. She just didn't like the direction the conversation was taking.

"Remember what they say about rules? That they have to be fair to you and everyone else, even people you don't like?" Celia asked. She seemed to be taking a ghoulish delight in Cheryl's distress. It was like everyone was getting fed up and gaining the courage to stand up to the princess.

"Well now, they're not being fair to *me*! If she can get them changed, then I too can get them changed, and I'm going to do just that—or die trying." Cheryl stuck out her pretty nose as she spat this out. Most of the girls looked at her with genuine shock before Celia burst into sarcastic laughter.

"You don't mean that, sweetie. By the way, the rules weren't fair to you at first. Now they're being changed and they're still unfair. You really are taking that 'things can never be done right unless you do them yourself' thing too far, don't you think?"

"Whatever!" Cheryl stomped off with two of the girls that always tagged after her. She was going to have to talk to Connor. She had the nagging feeling that if Latoya was going to be in the contest, she might be able to win. Someone would come up with some stupid stuff that no one understood and play on the sympathy of the judges. Previously, the only categories there had been in the pageant had been about the face, the shape, and how well one dressed. Now the contestants were going to be judged for other crazy stuff like their knowledge and interest in current affairs and empathy towards human conditions and circumstances. What in the hell was a human condition?

Cheryl didn't like things and people that made her think a lot. She only wanted to glow and smile and have the whole world fall into her lap.

She thought the idea of inner beauty was nonsense and stuff. There definitely was no way that anyone was going to ever say "Well, her face is kind of a mess, but she has real cute lungs." It was all balderdash. If you were cute, you were cute; if you weren't, then you weren't! It all seemed so simple and clear to Cheryl, and her beau totally agreed with her.

"We are going to put a stop to all than hon," he mumbled into her ear later that day during recess. He looked around furtively. Not even the members of his crew should hear him when he said that. For the kind of things that he wanted to pull, he used another crew—his *dad's*.

Cheryl knew all that. About the secret thing Connor's dad belonged to. It scared her, but she was getting used to it. She had been horrified about what had happened to poor Ned and his family—learning who was behind it and what their motives had been.

Ordinarily, she would also be the target of such attacks. They were mostly about race. Connor though, had assured her that as long as she was with him—and considering the whole princess thing and the fact that she was half Caucasian—she was safe. The same could not be said about Latoya Lami, whose parents were both black.

"We've had enough of that . . . thing and her nonsense." The way Connor wrinkled his face while he was searching for a word to describe Latoya scared Cheryl a little. For one nanosecond she thought of retracting and telling Connor to forget about the whole thing, but then she thought about the humiliation of being beat in the beauty contest by Latoya, of all things, and she became certain that she was for the idea of putting a stop to her nonsense.

"I hope no one is going to get killed . . . or badly hurt though." She squeezed Connor's hand as she said that.

"Of course, no one's getting killed. What do you think we are? Murderers?" Connor didn't seem very offended at the insinuation, but what worried Cheryl even more was the 'we' part of it. She wasn't exactly sure who was involved in Connor's dad and his band—only that they were quite dangerous.

As she made her way towards Miss. Hudson's office, the thought of Connor's dad and his gang kept nagging and nibbling away at her mind like a little rat.

8

What is the Use Anyway?

The day after Latoya's withdrawal from the student panel and her entry into the contest, the news making the rounds was that two of the sponsors that routinely used the Miss Grange Academyy contest to advertise had withdrawn. They were cosmetics manufacturers. Fortunately, Principal Fischer managed to get some mysterious donor who stood in the gap.

"All is not lost after all!" He had beamed pleasantly as he announced that to Miss Hudson.

"You look lost!" he said, looking at Miss Hudson with deep concern. She didn't seem to have understood the good news he had just told her. He wondered what had come over her lately. She just seemed so distracted and kind of scared.

"Huh?" Miss Hudson exclaimed absently. "No, I'm quite okay. That is very good news!"

Principal Fischer knew Miss Hudson well enough to be able to tell that something was definitely amiss. It was probably something at home that she didn't want to talk about. He was so preoccupied with the contest and worrying about everything going smoothly that he had been unable to notice much of the drama that was going on all around him.

"Should I get someone else to help you organize the event, Larisa?" he asked, his broad face creasing with concern.

Miss Hudson hastily flashed what she probably thought was a reassuring smile. It was forced, and that wasn't lost on Principal Fischer.

"No, I'm fine, really!" she said in the most cheerful voice she could manage. "I think it's just the excitement and stress getting to me, but I'll be fine!"

"Okay! If you say so." Principal Fischer let it go, but he made a mental note to keep a keen eye out and be sure that Miss Hudson was going to cope with organizing the event. It was only three weeks away. Nothing more could go wrong. Unknown to him, something was already going wrong that was going to throw the school into deep turmoil in a matter of hours.

*****

Dear Diary,
"What's the use anyway? I'm tired of trying. No one cares, and I'm tired of caring. This is where it should stop. I can't go on pretending that everything is okay. I'm tired of waking up and dragging myself to school and having everyone avoid me . . ."

Libby felt drained and exhausted as she made this entry into her diary. She was tired of the binge eating and the vomiting. Tired was all she felt every hour of every day. No one—not even the teachers—seemed concerned about the sharp shift in her behavior. They probably thought that she was only dealing with her parent's separation and she was soon going to get used to everything.

She just didn't want to go on that way anymore, but she felt so alone and weak. She didn't have the strength to do it all by herself. And her mother had become so grumpy and angry all the time. She seemed to use every chance to scold and quarrel about one thing or another. And Libby was the one that was usually on the receiving end. All her classmates gave her a wide berth, and none of the teachers seemed concerned. It seemed that what everyone cared about was the Miss Grange Academy Beauty Contest and who was going to be in or out. She was definitely out, and the world didn't care. She may as well get herself out of everything else—end it all.

With her dad gone, they had been forced to move into a smaller apartment. "You're a big girl now; you should help take care of the apartment. I can't be coming home to a messy house and a mess, mess, *mess* everywhere!" Her mother shouted every evening, even when the house was sparkling clean. Libby had given up trying to point out that she did the best she could do. She was trying. Her mother never listened anyway.

"So, you expect to sit around and be idle? Your father is not here to turn you into a spoiled little brat!" Whenever she mentioned her father, Libby always knew her mother was about to flip. Talking about her dad just turned some kind of switch inside her mum—one that turned her into someone that Libby no longer knew. There was something about the way she always said, "Your father isn't around." Perhaps that's what was really making her so angry.

That particular evening, Libby had tried as much as possible to ensure that there wouldn't be any reason for her mother to scold and shout. She had summoned the strength to tidy up the entire house after school. Sometimes her little brother made a mess. Libby had made sure that the toys had been picked up and neatly put away in the two toy boxes. And she made her mother's favorite meal, beef stew with carrots and eggplant. Libby had also made naan, the flat bread her mother loved so much and had taught her to make. She wanted the atmosphere to be right when she talked to her mother about the problem she had been fighting for so long. But the first thing her mother had done as soon as she came in through the door was ask why on earth the coffee table was so close to the door.

'Would it kill you to do something as small as that? Just moving the table where it's supposed to be?" she angrily asked. Libby had looked with surprise at her mother's angry face. What had she done to make her so mad? It just couldn't be about the table. Suddenly, Libby felt so tired . . . like she just wanted to lie down and never get up again. She just couldn't go on living.

Deep within her, Libby was scared by the very thought of doing what had crossed her mind at that moment. She wanted to live—to be happy—but this seemed like the end of the road. There just wasn't any way out. She just wished Ned had been around. Apart from her father, he had been the only person she could really open up to. Her other school friends were engrossed in competing with each other, each trying to prove that they came from a better family, were more beautiful, or better in class that the others.

Latoya had started being friendly and trying to strike up a conversation with her, but as much as a part of her wanted to reach out to her, another part just wanted to keep to herself. And now she just felt like it was time to give it all up. There was no need to go on.

Libby looked around her room. Then she decided to write something for Ned. He was probably alive and well somewhere on the planet. She would surely have heard if he had died or something. Perhaps they would meet again some day—in another life.

Ned,

I don't know where you are, but I'm sure you are still alive somewhere in this world. I really wish you were here now. Then I would never have to do what I'm about to do. I'm sorry I couldn't explain why I was so down that day, and I know you imagined I was angry with you or something. I just want you to know that you are the most wonderful person I have ever known. And I wish we could have been friends forever, but now it can only happen in another life. I have to do this. I can't take it anymore. My father went away, and my mother has turned into a total stranger. I can't live like this anymore. I hope you will understand some day and forgive me.

That was the note that was found on her laptop. It was still on, when her mother had come in the next morning to see why she wasn't up yet. It was Mr. Hepburn, the next-door neighbor, who called 911, as Libby's mum had too upset to do it.

The terrible news rocked the entire school with the intensity of an atom bomb. Everyone became headless chickens and ran around without a single idea of what should be done. No one could have imagined that such a thing could happen.

There was an air of gloom all round, and even Connor and his friends weren't their usual ribald and loud selves. For once, no one was mentioning the contest, and even Cheryl wasn't completely preoccupied with how highly she rated herself.

Everyone gathered in the common hall for Principal Fischer to make the announcement. He had a black ribbon on the lapel of his dark suit. He was one of those people with very readable body language. Everyone could clearly see just how profoundly it had all affected him.

"If only we knew how to stop and turn back the wheels of time, we would go back and right our many wrongs," he said in a low, sorrow-ful voice. It was clear that he somehow blamed himself for what had happened.

In the hall, it was as if poor Libby's ghost was hovering overhead, sneering at their presence—at the fact that now they cared so much, yet they had ignored her when she needed them to care. When their caring could have rescued her. There was a deep sense of guilt all around.

Latoya sat right in the front, where she was used to sitting. She thought of the time that she had casually mentioned Libby to Nimo. She had felt that she knew what Libby had been going through. She knew what it was to feel hurt and left out. She guessed that may have been quite close to what poor Libby had been going through. She dabbed her nose with her hankie and sniffed. She had been so engrossed in her wars with Cheryl that she didn't notice that there were worse problems around her.

"What has happened has happened," Principal Fischer said. "We just have to find a way to go through this, and emerge at the end of it with learned lessons and healed hearts."

Latoya noticed that Miss Hudson, standing beside Principal Fischer, had a faraway look on her face. It was as if she was trying to figure something out. She didn't look particularly sad, Latoya thought. Just very thoughtful.

Miss Hudson's unusual behavior hadn't been lost on Latoya. It was all so puzzling. Had she been her usual self,

Miss Hudson would have been very emotional and broken up at this time. It seemed unlikely, though, that the contest was going to go on as planned. This unexpected setback was definitely going to sound the death knell on it.

Latoya had no idea how closely her thoughts at that moment matched what was going on in Miss Hudson's mind. Miss Hudson was thinking, with a sense of relief, that the contest was now going to have to be cancelled. If that was going to be the case, then it was going to save her a lot of trouble. She wasn't sure she could do what was being demanded of her, and she was scared that when she failed, those that were demanding it of her were going to do something that was going to have a very drastic effect on the school and the entire community

9

The Final Farewell

Libby's mum had never been a regular church-goer. Of course, she always went for mass with her mother at the local Catholic church when she was much younger, but it had just been kind of a routine thing—go to church, sing the hymns, respond to whatever the priest said, listen to the sermon, and go back home. It had no noticeable effect on her whatsoever. The whole thing about looking up to God and depending on Him as everyone seemed to be telling her ever since her daughter's tragic death . . . well, it was something that other people did. She had always thought that she had it all together—that she could face and do anything in her life that needed to be done.

Perhaps the only reason she had been able to do that had been because her life had been without any major setbacks. She had been raised in a fairly comfortable home, and had sailed through school and college near the top of every class. There had been nothing that she could remember that she could call a difficulty. Soon after college, she had fallen in love, got married to who she thought was the perfect man,

66

and had three adorable children. Then everything started falling apart at the seams.

She looked wearily at the white coffin on the table at the front of the temple surrounded by swirls and gusts of incense. Libby had not been a confirmed Catholic, but her parents were. The church had agreed to conduct her requiem mass.

A few pews away, Eddie Knight, Libby's dad sat with his face set grimly as if it was carved from granite. As if to clearly demonstrate to Libby's mum just how apart he wanted them to be, he had insisted that Sam and Gertie, their other children sit with him, his two brothers, their wives, and the other relatives who had come for the funeral. Little Gertie was scared of strangers, and she had cried and fussed until she was allowed to go and sit near her mother.

Sam had obeyed, but he kept glancing over at his mother every so often, and it made her feel even more rotten than she already did. Libby . . . Elizabeth . . . Just like a flower, she had graced the world with her natural beauty and fragrance for only a brief time, before it became time for her to move on. Or had it been? Suzanne wished she had been more observant of and closer to her daughter. Then perhaps she wouldn't have done what she did. When her sister had discovered Libby's diary, it had been so heart wrenching for Suzanne. Perhaps Libby had written down all those things because there was no one she could talk to. Perhaps Suzanne should have encouraged her to be closer to their older relatives—to have more friends. But then, it had always seemed to her that Libby had so many friends. She had always been a happy, outgoing child. What could have gone wrong? A fresh wave of despair overcame Suzanne as the thoughts rushed through her mind, and she began to sob again.

The priests had completed the ritual they had been doing around the coffin and took their places on the seats placed near the altar. Mr. Grey, one of the teachers from Grange Academy, walked over to the coffin and bowed slightly before picking up the microphone. He was the master of ceremony for the grim occasion.

"For the short time that they are allowed by God to be with us," Mr. Grey began solemnly, "flowers are able to bring so much joy into our lives. The glow of their beauty, the sweetness of the nectar within them, and the fragrance of their perfume is more than most other objects have to offer. Here today, we are gathered to appreciate and celebrate the joy that one such flower filled our lives with." He paused for a couple of seconds. "I know that 'celebrate' is not quite the word to use at such a gathering, but yes, I will use it just the same, for having had the opportunity to get to know such a wonderful and exceptional person is something that can only be celebrated. I was not yet part of Grange Academyy when Libby joined, but for all the time I knew her, she was always full of life and beauty. She exuded such a fragrance and contained such sweetness within her that whoever got to know her could never go untouched by the power of that interaction . . ."

Far from offering her any comfort, each of Mr. Grey's words was like a hot coal in the open wound of her grief. She just wanted to scream and throw herself around and tear at her clothes without caring what anyone thought.

Her daughter's death was the worst thing she had ever had to cope with. She glanced over at her husband as he sat looking straight ahead with an expressionless face. Suzanne knew that Eddie blamed her and trying hard to hold his anger in. She wished they could sit beside each other, hold hands, and offer comfort to each other during this difficult period. Which of them was to blame? Both of them equally?

"I'm so sorry, baby . . . so sorry," Suzanne whispered to herself. She glanced towards the right side of the church where Libby's former school mates were sitting. About eight of Libby's former classmates sat closer to the coffin because they were the pall bearers. All were quiet in their grey and white uniforms. But her baby would no longer be needing her uniform. She had always been so excited about school. She had always done everything with so much enthusiasm. Always such a loving, sunny kid . . . what had happened? Why hadn't she, her very own mother, not seen it coming?

Most of those in attendance were parents whose children were studying at Grange Academy. Suzanne had met most of them during school functions and PTA meetings. Sam was in grade four, and there was no doubt that she was going to see a lot more of them in future, unless Eddie decided to take the other children from her. No, she was not going to allow it. She needed Sam and Gertie with her. She was going to put up a fight; she was never going to allow him or anyone else to take them away from her *ever*. She had lost one of her babies, but God help anyone who ever tried to get the others away from her.

Everyone Deserves
a Break

The festive mood around Grange Academyy had been building up for quite a few weeks. before the actual event. The date of the contest had been changed when Libby died. "Trees lose all their leaves in fall and regain them in spring," said Principal Fischer, who'd made a tremendous effort to strike up some cheer when he made that announcement. "It's the circle of life—loss and gain. Let us step right out and see what we shall gain in return for the loss we have suffered!" he had urged them on.

Miss Hudson was no longer in charge, though. Mrs. Proctor had taken over and was the breath of life that the contest needed. It was announced that Miss. Hudson had taken sick leave and would not be coming back to school for some time. Later, there was a notice on the board outside the library that said Miss Hudson had been admitted to hospital, and it suggested that they say a word of prayer for her quick recovery.

The event had turned into a kind of festival, lasting an entire week, instead of a one-day event as it had previously been. More sponsors had eventually invested in the contest thanks to Principal Fischer's lobbying, and it was going to be better than ever. As part of the event, the participating students had visited children's homes and special schools around the state to familiarize themselves with children who were different from them. That too, was a new idea that Miss. Hudson had introduced, but Cheryl openly detested it. "Why do I have to be put through all this?!" she had shrilled to anyone who would listen. "Why can't we just get on with the contest? I'm the winner anyway. They might as well crown me now. I don't have to go and talk to drooling dummies and mutes." Nimo looked at her with disbelief and shook her head when she heard this. She sometimes wondered why she chose to be around Cheryl at all. True, she was a traditional princess, very pretty and all that, but she was one person who could really get under anyone's skin.

"Do you realize what you're saying?!" Nimo couldn't help asking.

"What!" Cheryl crossed her arms across her chest and looked at her defiantly "I have the right to say what I feel." Nimo shook her head and started walking away.

"Let her go," one of Cheryl's closest friends said out loud. "Always sympathizing with people of her class." Nimo clenched her fists and fought down the urge to turn around and confront her. She knew it could only lead to an unpleasant scene, and so she just decided to let it go. She felt so sorry for having preferred Cheryl to Latoya. It was obvious that Cheryl was someone who could hurt as she wished, without caring how other people felt. It certainly was the time for their friendship to end. Her distaste for Cheryl would perhaps have gone deeper, had she been aware of what

Cheryl had in mind with her beau Connor. No one could guess what kind of monster really lived under that perfect, Barbie doll face.

*****

The remaining five contestants were allowed to choose someone to escort them to the final contest—a friend or family member. Latoya, incredibly, looked beautiful! It was the only way you could describe her. She had on a pale green sequined bolero over a beige flowing ball gown that came to her ankles. The designer, none other than Maya, had made the gown in such a way as to complement Latoya's figure. Her luxurious hair had been relaxed and teased into a curly do, caught up with clasps at the nape of her neck. The eye makeup did something real nice her eyes. But what made her most beautiful seemed to come from deep inside her. There was something about her that no one else could clearly define—something that seemed to come from within her.

What no one noticed were the fiery glances Cheryl was sending Latoya's way ever so often. To be fair, Cheryl was one person that could be described as flawlessly beautiful, even at thirteen. Despite all that, she had this aura of ugliness around her. This was perhaps because of her arrogant nature. The ill feelings and bad thoughts that she always seemed to harbor against everyone else.

After the contestants had been questioned about a number of different issues. Latoya's confident and intelligent answers impressed not just the judges but most of the audience. Just the same way Cheryl's arrogance and impatience came out so obviously in the answers she gave. Although a lot of people applauded her, it was obvious that the judges were not impressed. Despite all that, no one thought anyone but

Batebe Cheryl Tate could be Miss Grange Academy. After clarifying the criteria used to reach the decision, the leading judge announced the winner. "I am delighted to announce that this year's Miss Grange Elementary is . . . LATOYA GRACE LAMI!!!"

Some of Cheryl's fans actually started cheering before they realized what had happened. Cheryl herself had started to rise from her chair before stopping short in shock. There was a pregnant pause before the crowd exploded into the wildest cheers you could ever imagine.

"To be honest, I didn't expect to get to the finals of this pageant . . . and I certainly didn't expect to be the winner," Toya started her speech after being crowned. "I am very grateful to Maya a good family friend, who helped me to realize that we are all beautiful . . . all of us, *everyone*. If only people would look past what they see at first glance. Everyone deserves a break, and everyone deserves to be accepted as they are. I would like to also thank my parents and my many, many friends who have been so supportive. And I would also like to thank my competition—especially Cheryl, who I hope I shall still be good friends with, for helping me to struggle and achieve this. The world belongs to everyone, and everyone is meant to be here. There is enough space for everyone. It is wrong for anyone to see themselves as more deserving of life, love and happiness than anyone else . . ."

In the deathly quiet crowd, both Mr. and Mrs. Lami couldn't stop their tears from flowing. Even Howie sniffled a bit as he looked around with a *Hey, that's my sister* grin on his face. Some of the students sniggered with amusement when they noticed Cheryl, her parents, and some other people they had come with hastily leaving the hall.

Just then, there was a tremendous explosion. The lights went off and darkness engulfed everything. The entire building shook on its foundation, like it was about to tip over and stand on its roof. It took a few long minutes for people to realize that the world had just ended, and all hell had just broken loose.

Then there was pandemonium. People started running all over the place, some stepping onto and over others that had fallen down. Soon the air was filled with screams and the wails of ambulances and police vehicles as they rushed to Grange Academy.

******

The happenings at Grange Academy were breaking news on every news station. Nothing else was broadcast for a long time to come on the local TV stations. The number of casualties kept being updated. Several students and parents and other guests were seriously injured in the attack. There had been five fatalities; three students, a parent, and a guest. Soon, reports of arrests started coming in. Gregory was the first to be arrested, alongside his son,Connor, and six other men that were employees at the convenience stores Mr. Haus owned. They all were members of a kind of crime 'family' involved in a lot of illegal activities.

At the behest of his son, Mr. Haus had set out to stop the pageant. When they couldn't intimidate Miss Hudson by threatening to burn down her house if she didn't somehow stop the event, they went ahead and planted explosives on the school grounds and set them off. Apparently, Cheryl and her parents had been warned to leave just before the explosives were set off.

It was an act of hate, but it drew people closer. Latoya and her family had escaped with minor injuries, luckily, and they joined the entire state in mourning.

As they clung to each other and drew comfort from the diversity of their backgrounds, people were learning the lesson they had been taught the hard way: the devastation that hate and intolerance cause. The unnecessary pain that results when people can't simply accept who others are. That the world would be a much better, happier place if everyone saw the beauty in everyone else, and accepted each other for whatever they were created as. Latoya Lami's story and her speech shortly before the unfortunate tragedy was repeated everywhere in the media and quoted by a number of papers …and people. Everyone referred to her as The Grange Academy beauty queen.

It was clear that a lot of people had learned a lesson that they were going to have to live with, as they found their footing again—as they moved on from the fall and winter, full of mistakes, to the happier times that spring and summer were sure to bring their way.

THE END